Latkes, Latkes Good to Eat

A CHANUKAH STORY
by Naomi Howland

CLARION BOOKS/NEW YORK

Clarion Books
a Houghton Mifflin Company imprint
215 Park Avenue South, New York, NY 10003
Copyright © 1999 by Naomi Howland
Type is 14/18 Palatino.
The illustrations for this book were executed in gouache and colored pencil
on Arches hot press paper.
Book design by Carol Goldenberg.

For information about permission to reproduce selections from this book,
write to Permissions, Houghton Mifflin Company, 215 Park Avenue South,
New York, NY 10003.
Printed in the USA.

Library of Congress Cataloging-in-Publication Data
Howland, Naomi.
Latkes, latkes, good to eat / by Naomi Howland.
p. cm.
Summary: In an old Russian village, Sadie and her brothers are poor and hungry until an old woman gives
Sadie a frying pan that will make potato pancakes until it hears the magic words that make it stop.
ISBN 0-395-89903-6
[1. Fairy tales. 2. Magic—Fiction. 3. Hanukkah—Fiction. 4. Jews—Russia—Fiction.]
I. Title.
PZ8.H845Lat   1999
[E]—dc21   97-50616
CIP
AC

WOZ 10 9 8 7 6 5

For my own latke lovers,
Susannah, Juliet, and Sam

Once, on the outskirts of a tiny village, a girl named Sadie lived with her four little brothers, Herschel, Hillel, Hayim, and the baby, Max. Their mama lived there too, but she was away helping Aunt Rose with her new baby.

The family was so poor that the one coin in Sadie's purse never had another coin to keep it company. Their house was so drafty, the wind whistled through it like a train going to Moscow. And they were always hungry.

This year, the first night of Chanukah was the coldest night yet,
and the snow was deep.

Sadie said, "Boys, go out and gather some firewood."

"It's too cold outside," Herschel said. "You go." He pushed Hillel to
the door.

"It's too dark outside," Hillel complained. "You go." He pulled Hayim to the door.

"But wood is so heavy," Hayim whined. "You go." He pointed to Herschel.

Sadie sighed. "I will get the wood. Watch the baby until I return."

Sadie's boots sank into the new snow. She walked from tree to tree picking up fallen branches. An hour passed; it got colder and darker and a bitter wind began to blow.

At last, Sadie packed up the wood and turned to go home.

Suddenly, a twig snapped. Sadie whirled around to see a bent old woman standing before her. The woman's face was as creased and lined as a bit of wrinkled cloth.

The old woman sneezed. "Achooo!"

"Bless you, Tante," Sadie said. She noticed the old woman's shoulders trembling. Her coat was shabby and thin. "Are you cold?"

"Oh, I am, dear," said the old woman, shivering. "And I have no more firewood." She blew on her hands to warm them.

Sadie didn't hesitate. "Please take this wood for your fire," she said. She piled all the wood she had gathered into the old woman's sack.

"Thank you," said the old woman. "You are a kind child. Now I have a gift for you." She unhooked a frying pan from her belt. "When you are hungry tonight, put this pan on the stove and say these words:

"Latkes, latkes, good to eat.
Cook me up a Chanukah treat!

When you are not hungry anymore, say, *'A great miracle happened here!'"*

"Thank you, Tante," Sadie said.

"Never forget the words I have taught you," warned the old woman. "Keep them a secret. Only you may use my gift." With that she hobbled off into the forest.

Sadie ran home. "Quickly, boys, let's light the menorah," she said. "I have a surprise."

As soon as they had said the blessing and lit the first candles, Herschel asked, "What's the surprise?"

"And where is our wood?" asked Hillel.

"I met an old woman in the forest," Sadie explained. "I gave her the wood because she was so cold. And she gave me this frying pan."

"What? A frying pan?" cried Herschel. "We don't even have a fire!"

"We don't have any food," Hayim complained.

"Just watch," said Sadie. She put the pan on the cold stove and whispered the old woman's words:

> *"Latkes, latkes, good to eat.*
> *Cook me up a Chanukah treat!"*

At that moment a fire danced up under the frying pan. Right away five golden latkes sizzled in oil.

The four little boys crowded around the stove.

"How did you do that?" asked Herschel.

"The old woman told me not to tell," answered Sadie. As soon as she put the latkes on their plates, another five latkes sputtered in the pan.

"Can I try?" asked Hillel.

"No, let me." Hayim pushed his brothers aside.

"No," said Sadie. "Only I can use the frying pan."

When the plates were heaped high with latkes, Sadie whispered, *"A great miracle happened here!"* And the magic frying pan stopped cooking just . . . like . . . that!

They ate and ate until their stomachs were full.

The next night, after Sadie and her brothers lit their menorah, Sadie set the frying pan on the stove. In a hushed voice she repeated the words,

> *"Latkes, latkes, good to eat.*
> *Cook me up a Chanukah treat!"*

Immediately, a fire glowed under the pan, where five delicious latkes were sizzling.

When the plates were heaped high, Sadie said softly, *"A great miracle happened here!"* The frying pan stopped cooking just . . . like . . . that!

Each night of Chanukah the children sat down to another tasty dinner of potato pancakes. Then, the afternoon of the eighth night, Sadie put on her shawl. "I am going to find the old woman and invite her to eat latkes with us tonight," she said. "I will cook them when I get back. Take care of the baby and be good boys. And don't touch the frying pan!"

All together the brothers nodded their heads and solemnly said, "We promise."

Only a minute after Sadie had closed the door, Herschel boasted, "I heard the secret words."

"You did not," said Hillel. "And we aren't supposed to touch the frying pan."

"I did too," said Herschel.

"We could eat just a few latkes," said Hayim. "Sadie won't know."

Max, the baby, said, "Latkes! Latkes!"

The boys looked at Herschel. Herschel looked at the pan. "It's easy to use the frying pan," he said. "Just watch." He put the frying pan on the stove and said,

> *"Latkes, latkes, good to eat.*
> *Cook me up a Chanukah treat!"*

The stove lit itself with a bright flame. At once the frying pan was filled with five latkes sputtering in oil.

When the latkes were hot and golden, Herschel said, "Great! Here a miracle happened."

The frying pan began cooking five more latkes, with tender centers and crisp lacy edges.

"We have enough, brother," said Hillel. But the frying pan kept on cooking. The little boys piled their plates high with latkes.

"Here great miracles happened?" tried Herschel. The frying pan cooked up five more luscious, brown-flecked latkes.

The four brothers ate fast, but the frying pan cooked faster. Soon they had filled every dish, all the mixing bowls, and the washtub with steaming hot latkes.

Hayim cried, "Stop, frying pan!" But the frying pan cooked up five more latkes, savory and salty.

"Happy green miracles here!" Max yelled. But the pan kept cooking. The boys hid latkes in the cupboard and under the bed. They fed latkes to the cat.

Soon latkes were spilling out the door. The smell of potatoes and onions and oil floated through the village. The shoemaker stopped cobbling to sniff. The fishmonger, holding a fresh carp, paused to breathe in the fragrance. The village gossip even stopped talking long enough to inhale the aroma of Chanukah cooking.

Meanwhile, Sadie had walked deep into the blue-shadowed forest. "Tante! Tante!" she called, over and over, but there was no answer. Where could the old woman be? Soon the sun would go down, and Sadie needed to be home by dark to light the menorah. Now she wasn't sure she even knew the way home.

Bony branches scratched the sky. Sadie shivered. "Taaante!" she called again. The wind whistled through the dark trees. It carried a tantalizing aroma.

There was a rustle of dry leaves and the old woman appeared. Before Sadie could say a word, the old woman held up her hand for silence and sniffed the air.

Sadie, too, breathed deeply. Potatoes . . . onions . . . oil. Latkes! "Oh, no!" she cried. Following her nose, she began to run, with the old woman close behind.

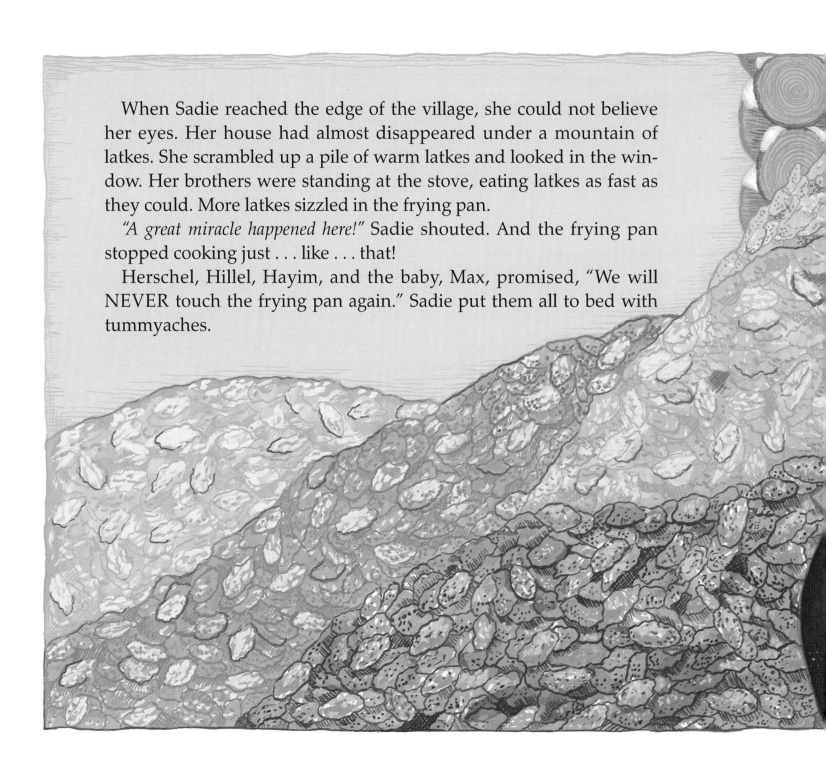

When Sadie reached the edge of the village, she could not believe her eyes. Her house had almost disappeared under a mountain of latkes. She scrambled up a pile of warm latkes and looked in the window. Her brothers were standing at the stove, eating latkes as fast as they could. More latkes sizzled in the frying pan.

"A great miracle happened here!" Sadie shouted. And the frying pan stopped cooking just . . . like . . . that!

Herschel, Hillel, Hayim, and the baby, Max, promised, "We will NEVER touch the frying pan again." Sadie put them all to bed with tummyaches.

"But what will we do with all these latkes?" she wondered.
"I could carry them away," said the village porter.
"I could sweep them up," said the broom seller.
"We could eat them," said someone else. It was Mama—home from helping Aunt Rose!
"We'll have a Chanukah feast!" said Sadie. "Everyone is invited."

What a party the village had that night! There was singing and dancing and dreidel playing, and of course there were latkes— golden, tongue-burning hot, tender yet crisp, lacy, luscious, brown-flecked, savory, salty, scrumptious latkes to eat.

30

And no one in the tiny village was ever hungry on Chanukah again.

Sadie's Latkes

Sadie would have made latkes (say LOT-kuz) this way if she hadn't had a magic frying pan. This recipe makes about a dozen $3\frac{1}{2}''$ pancakes. You can double the recipe and have twice as many scrumptious latkes to eat. Be sure to have an adult help you.

3 large potatoes (about 1 pound)
2 eggs
$\frac{1}{4}$ cup finely chopped onion
1 tablespoon finely chopped parsley

$\frac{1}{2}$ teaspoon salt
$\frac{1}{8}$ teaspoon pepper
3 tablespoons flour
vegetable oil

1. Peel the potatoes and rinse them in cold water. Grate very fine. Place the grated potatoes in a colander and run cold water over them. (This will keep the potatoes from turning dark.) Using your hands, squeeze out all the water.
2. In a large bowl, beat the eggs. Add the onion, parsley, salt, pepper, and flour. Stir. Add grated potatoes and mix well.
3. Heat a small amount of oil to sizzling in a large frying pan. Drop pancake mixture by the soupspoonful into oil and flatten slightly. Cook until golden brown underneath, turn, and cook on the other side till browned.
4. Eat while still tender but crisp! Latkes are traditionally served with applesauce and/or sour cream.

A Note

Chanukah, the Jewish Festival of Lights, commemorates the fight for religious freedom by a small band of Jews in 165 B.C. After their victory, the Jews went to rekindle the Eternal Light in their Temple. There was only enough oil to burn for one day. Miraculously it burned for eight days, enough time for the Jews to make more oil and keep the Eternal Light burning.

Jews light candles in a *menorah* or *chanukiah* for eight nights as a reminder of those events. Foods cooked in oil, such as latkes and jelly doughnuts, also remind people of the miracle of Chanukah.

During Chanukah, games are played with a *dreidel*, a top with Hebrew letters written on its four sides. In Israel, the letters are *Nun, Gimel, He, Pe,* which stand for the sentence *Nes Gadol Hayah Po,* "A great miracle happened here." Outside of Israel, the letters are *Nun, Gimel, He, Shin,* which stand for "A great miracle happened there."

Tante means "aunt" in Yiddish. Sadie uses the word as a term of respect.